Saving Sammy

Eric Walters

ILLUSTRATED BY **Amy Meissner**

Saving Sammy

Eric Walters
ILLUSTRATED BY Amy Meissner

ORCA BOOK PUBLISHERS

Library and Archives Canada Cataloguing in Publication

Walters, Eric, 1957-, author
Saving Sammy / Eric Walters ;
illustrated by Amy Meissner.
(Orca echoes)

Issued in print and electronic formats.
ISBN 978-1-4598-0499-9 (pbk.).--ISBN 978-1-4598-0500-2 (pdf).
ISBN 978-1-4598-0501-9 (epub)

1. Beavers--Juvenile fiction. I. Meissner, Amy, illustrator
II. Title. III. Series: Orca echoes
PS8595.A598S29 2014   jC813'.54   C2013-906855-4
C2013-906856-2

First published in the United States, 2014
Library of Congress Control Number: 2013955770

Summary: Morgan learns to care for a baby beaver that is washed
into her backyard by floodwaters.

Orca Book Publishers gratefully acknowledges the support for its publishing programs
provided by the following agencies: the Government of Canada through the Canada Book Fund
and the Canada Council for the Arts, and the Province of British Columbia
through the BC Arts Council and the Book Publishing Tax Credit.

MIX
Paper from
responsible sources
FSC® C004071

*Orca Book Publishers is dedicated to preserving the environment and
has printed this book on Forest Stewardship Council® certified paper.*

Cover artwork and interior illustrations by Amy Meissner

ORCA BOOK PUBLISHERS
PO Box 5626, STN. B
Victoria, BC Canada
v8R 6s4

ORCA BOOK PUBLISHERS
PO Box 468
Custer, WA USA
98240-0468

www.orcabook.com
Printed and bound in Canada.

17 16 15 14 • 4 3 2 1

*For the Monkman family, who shared
the story of rescuing Sammy from behind
their house by the river. — EW*

With many thanks to Aimee D. — ACM

Chapter One

Morgan opened one eye and listened closely. It wasn't what she heard but what she *didn't* hear that made her happy. There was no sound of rain on the roof. For days it had been raining. Her father had joked that maybe it was time to start building an ark and gathering animals two by two. It was a joke, but when you lived right beside a flooding river, it was only a small joke. Morgan was much more concerned about the flooding than she'd ever let on.

She climbed out of bed and looked out the window. The river had retreated. It was still there, rough, white and wide, but it was no longer running through the corner of their backyard. Still, there was

proof that it had once been there. The back fence was covered in branches that had been snagged as the floodwaters raced across their property.

The family dogs were already outside, running and playing, happy to be allowed in the backyard again. Rylee—only a year old—was running around in circles as though he was herding imaginary sheep. Morgan was sure that's what Australian shepherds dreamed of. Shire, a Lab, was much older and slower, but this morning he was moving faster than usual. They both looked like they were having fun exploring the new smells from objects left behind by the floodwaters.

For Morgan, the river's retreat meant work. She and her parents would have to clean up the mess. Branches were strewn everywhere around the yard. She wouldn't complain because she knew there had been years when the floods were worse. The previous spring, the melting snow and ice had swollen the river so much that it lapped at the back porch. Her parents had been really worried. They'd thought they might even have to leave the house behind and move in with her grandparents until the river returned to normal.

Shire started baying. Big loud barks kept coming from deep in his chest. That wasn't like him. He was usually so quiet and well behaved. He stood at the edge of the property, right by the fence, and continued to call out. His barking attracted Rylee, who stopped herding and went over to see for himself. There had to be something out there.

Morgan peered through the glass, trying to see what was bothering Shire. Living out in the country, she had often seen wild animals wander across their property. Deer were common, but she'd also seen foxes, rabbits, and even a black bear come through the yard. She scanned the whole area but couldn't see anything. Morgan knew that didn't mean there wasn't something out there. The dogs could smell what she couldn't see. Shire continued to bark. Whatever it was, Morgan needed to investigate.

Chapter Two

Morgan got dressed and hurried down the stairs. Her mother was by the sink, washing dishes, and her father was at the stove, making breakfast. That was their routine. One did the cooking and the other did the cleanup. Both were good cooks, but Morgan's father was *much* better at making a mess. They always joked that he needed three pots and a kettle just to boil water.

"Good morning, Sunshine," Morgan's father said.

"Morning, Dad, good morning, Mom."

Her mother gave her a kiss on the forehead. "I didn't expect to see you up this early on a Saturday. Did Shire wake you up?"

"I was up anyway," she said. "The rain *not* falling against the window was so loud."

Morgan's father laughed. "That silence was like music to my ears."

They didn't talk much about what could have happened the previous year. Morgan's best friend, Emily—who lived just down the river from them— had been flooded out that spring. Her family was back in their home now, but for months they had had to live elsewhere while their house was being repaired. Most of the year, Morgan loved having her window open at night and listening to the sound of the river meandering by so close. Close was wonderful. *Too* close was not.

"I wonder what was bothering Shire this morning," her mother said.

"Probably smelled something in the distance," her father said. "He's old, but his nose still works well."

Shire had been part of their family since before Morgan was born, so she didn't know life without him.

He joined them on family holidays. At mealtimes, he sat politely off to the side, hoping somebody tossed him a scrap. On Christmas mornings, he poked his nose into the wrappings that littered the floor. Morgan's parents told her tales about Shire giving up his doggie bed to sleep on the floor beside her crib. How she'd learned to walk by holding onto his fur while Shire moved slowly along, never complaining. Morgan knew he was getting older, but bringing in the new young dog, Rylee, had seemed to make Shire younger as well.

"Morgan, can you call the dogs in for their breakfast before we have ours?" her mother asked.

The two bowls sat on the counter, already filled with food. Morgan put them on the floor and opened the door.

"Shire and Rylee, come on! Breakfast is served!" she called out.

Rylee didn't need a second invitation. He leaped up onto the porch and through the door, practically

bowling Morgan over in his rush to get to the food. But Shire wasn't coming. He *was* getting a little hard of hearing. She called again. This time he turned to look at her, but he still didn't come. Instead he sat on the ground, staring off into the distance.

"Shire isn't coming," Morgan said.

"It's not like him to turn down a meal," her father said.

"It's not like *any* of the males in this family to turn down a meal," her mother teased. "Not that either of you couldn't afford to skip a meal every now and again."

"Hey, hey, you can poke fun at me if you want, but not at Shire," her father said.

Shire had added some weight over the years, and he certainly wasn't as quick or energetic as he once had been. Still, he was a healthy dog who loved going for walks and chasing a ball. With Rylee around, he could never quite get to the ball first, so they tossed a second one just for him.

Morgan scooped up Shire's bowl and placed it on the counter before Rylee could get at it. Maybe Shire could afford to skip a meal, but Rylee didn't need to have two of them.

"I'm going out to see him," Morgan said.

"I think I'll come with you," her mother said.

They both slipped on their shoes and slipped out the door. Crossing the porch and stepping down, they could see the tracks created by floodwaters. Grass had been flattened, and the river had left behind twigs and branches and silt and sand.

"Hello, boy, how are you doing?" Morgan called out.

Shire turned around. He didn't move but answered with a wagging tail and a smile. Morgan *loved* that Shire always seemed to be smiling. Even better, he always made her smile back.

"What's wrong, boy, aren't you hungry for breakfast? I could bring it out here if you—" She stopped.

There was something on the ground between Shire's two outstretched front paws. It was small, black and furry. It was an animal!

Chapter Three

Morgan blinked hard. Maybe it was nothing. No, there it was, a small tuft of black fur that blended into Shire's coat.

"Mom, he has something."

"I see that," her mother said. "I just don't know what I'm seeing."

The animal wasn't much bigger than one of Shire's paws. Its fur was slicked down and soaking wet.

"What is it?" Morgan asked.

"It could be a muskrat or baby skunk or even a raccoon. I can't tell…it's so small."

"Is it…is it…alive?" Morgan asked.

"I guess there's only one way to find out."

Carefully, her mother reached down toward the animal. It moved! It was alive!

It looked up at them with little brown eyes, opened its mouth and let out a tiny squeak. It squeaked again and then Shire started to whine softly.

"Poor little baby," her mother said.

Morgan reached down and gently placed her hand on the animal's back. "It's trembling. It must be scared."

"Or cold," her mother said.

"Or both. I'd be cold too if I was out here soaking wet. I'd also be scared if I didn't have anybody to look after me."

"I suppose Shire thinks he's looking after it," her mother said.

"But I wonder where its parents are?"

Morgan and her mother looked all around. No other animals were in sight.

"I know that when a baby bird falls from its nest, the parents stay close to watch over it," her mother said.

"But this isn't a baby bird, and I don't see any nest," Morgan said.

"They could be close by and are afraid to come here because of us and the dogs."

"What do we do?" Morgan asked.

"We could go inside for a while and bring Shire with us."

"And just leave it alone?"

"We can watch from the window to make sure it's safe. Then maybe the parents will come get their baby. Would that be all right?" her mother asked.

It felt wrong to just leave it alone, but Morgan knew her mother was right. She nodded.

"Come on, Shire," Morgan said as they got up.

Shire didn't want to leave either. He stayed there, protecting the baby.

Morgan's mother took Shire by the collar and led the dog away. Shire wasn't happy and struggled, looking back at the little bundle of fur. Then there was a cry—it sounded almost like a baby's cry—and

all three of them stopped and turned around. It cried again, this time louder.

"It's calling for us…or Shire," Morgan said.

"Or its parents," her mother said. "We have to give them a chance."

Morgan nodded, and the three of them continued into the house, closing the door behind them.

"What is it?" Morgan's father asked.

"It's a baby animal," her mother answered.

"What sort of animal?" he asked.

"We're not really sure, but we're going to leave it alone for a while to see if its parents will come and get it."

"That's the best thing to do."

Five sets of eyes—three human and two dog—stared out through the glass toward the river, watching and waiting.

Chapter Four

Shire whined ever so softly. Morgan felt like whining too, but stayed quiet and tried to be patient. It wasn't easy to be either.

"How much longer?" her father asked.

Morgan wondered the same thing.

"It's been ten minutes," her mother said. "I think if the parents were close, they would have come by now."

"Let's go out then," her father said. "But we'll leave the dogs inside."

Morgan knew that Shire wouldn't be happy, so she took his bowl off the counter and put it down in front of him. Both Shire and Rylee started eating from Shire's bowl.

Morgan and her parents went outside. They hadn't gone more than a few feet when they heard Shire barking and pawing at the door.

"We'll be back soon, boy!" Morgan called over her shoulder.

The little ball of fur was still lying in the grass. It called out to them—a mournful cry. Did it sound weaker now? They bent down, surrounding the animal and protecting it. It looked up at them, its eyes bright, and called out again.

"It's shaking," Morgan's father said.

Morgan pulled off her bright yellow jacket and tucked it around the baby.

"How do you think it got here?" her mother asked.

"It could have been washed up here by the floodwaters," her father said.

"But wouldn't it have drowned?" Morgan asked.

"It looks like it's half drowned as it is."

"I'm still not even sure what type of animal it is," her mother said.

"Me neither. It's so young that I can't tell."

"Can I pick it up?" Morgan asked.

Neither parent answered right away. "Just be gentle and careful," her mother finally said.

Morgan slipped her hand beneath the little ball of fur. As she picked it up, a big flat tail popped out from beneath it.

"It's a beaver!" she exclaimed. "A baby beaver!"

"That explains why it didn't drown," her father said. "It's a baby, but it's still a beaver."

Morgan pulled the baby close, and it nuzzled into her arm.

"The floodwaters must have washed it out of its den," Morgan's mother said.

"Should we try to take it back?" Morgan asked.

"There are dens all along the river," her father said. "There's no telling how far it was washed."

"So what do we do?" Morgan asked.

"For starters, let's bring it inside where it's warmer," her mother suggested.

They walked toward the house, and Shire began to bark even louder, pawing and pressing against the door. The food had distracted him, but he hadn't forgotten. As they entered, he pressed his nose right up to the little beaver.

"It's okay, boy," Morgan said. "It's safe now."

The beaver began to cry again, and Shire whined in response.

"Do you think it's hungry?" Morgan asked.

"I wouldn't be surprised. It was probably out there all night," her mother said.

"I can warm up some milk," her father said. "But it's so young, how will it ever take the milk?"

"I have an idea." Her mother left the room and came back carrying a box. Morgan recognized it instantly. It was her memory box, the place where her parents kept special things from when she was younger. What would they need in there? Her mother pulled out a small plastic baby bottle.

"This was yours when you were a baby. Do you mind if we use it for *this* baby?"

"Of course not!" Morgan exclaimed.

They heated some milk on the stove. Morgan's father tested a drop on his wrist to make sure it was warm and not hot. Her mother poured the milk out of the pot and into the bottle. She handed it to Morgan.

"I think you should do the feeding."

"Me?"

"It's either you or Shire, and I don't know if he could hold the bottle," her father said.

Morgan sat down on a kitchen chair. She cradled the baby beaver in her arm, wrapped in her jacket. The animal looked up at her with shiny black eyes. It didn't look scared anymore and had stopped shaking. As it dried, the black fur was becoming browner. Shire came over and put his head on Morgan's lap so that his nose nuzzled the baby. She placed the bottle by the baby's mouth, but it didn't seem to know what to do.

"Just squeeze the bottle a little," her mother said, "so a few drops of milk come out."

A bit of milk dribbled onto the baby's mouth. It made a chirping sound and then latched on to the bottle, holding it with its front paws. Morgan saw small bubbles appear in the bottle, and she could hear the beaver drinking. She felt like crying out for joy, but she didn't. She just held the baby and let it drink.

"It's working," her mother said softly. "It's working." Her parents looked as happy as Morgan felt.

"He's warm and dry and he's eating," her father said. "Now there's only one more thing to do."

"What's that?" Morgan asked.

"He needs a name."

"Is it even a *he*?" her mother asked.

"I'm not sure. It could be a baby girl, so there's only one safe thing to do—pick a name that could work for both a boy and a girl," he suggested.

"I know the perfect name," Morgan said.

"You do?" they asked at the same time.

"Yes. This is Sammy."

Chapter Five

Morgan's father put down the phone. "I'm afraid there's nobody from animal control who can come out right now," he said. "They're handling emergency calls."

"But isn't this an emergency?" Morgan asked.

"I guess not," he said. "They said they'd send somebody out, but it won't be until tomorrow at the earliest."

"So what are we going to do until then?" Morgan asked.

"I guess the same things we're doing now," her mother said. "They seem to be working."

Sammy slurped down the milk in the first bottle and then moved on to a second. Sammy was a *very* hungry baby. Of course, it seemed like half of the milk was going onto his fur instead of into his mouth. That made Shire even happier to lick the baby.

Both dogs had been let out, and Rylee was content to stay in the backyard and run. Not Shire though. He insisted on coming right back in. It was like he thought he was the mother or the father—or at least an uncle or aunt.

As Sammy got warmer, drier and better fed, he became more active. He waddled across the floor, his broad beaver tail trailing behind as he followed Shire around the room. Apparently, Shire wasn't the only one who thought they were related.

"He certainly is cute," Morgan's father said.

"He is," her mother agreed. "I've never seen a baby beaver before."

"I think that's because they're kept in their den until they're much older than this," he said.

"Don't beavers usually have a whole litter of babies?" Morgan asked.

"I did some research online when you were feeding Sammy," her mother said. "There are usually between two and eight in the litter."

Both of her parents knew what Morgan was thinking—what about the other kits in the litter?

"It might have been only Sammy that was washed away," her father said.

"Or the whole lodge could have been destroyed. What if they're all out there, just like Sammy, scared and hungry?" Morgan looked like she was going to cry.

Her mother put a hand on her shoulder. "How about if we leave your father to watch Sammy and you and I take a walk down by the river?"

"That would be wonderful! Can we take Shire with us? After all, he was the one who found Sammy."

"We can try. I just don't know if he'll be willing to leave Sammy here."

Morgan and her mother put on their boots and coats. It was spring but still chilly. Too chilly for a little beaver to be out by itself. Morgan's father held Sammy in his arms, and they coaxed Shire out the door with them. Rylee didn't need any encouragement as he raced forward. That dog only knew full speed ahead.

They went through the gate and walked toward the river. The floodwaters had receded even farther throughout the day. The river was still high but much lower and closer to its usual run. Without talking, they started upstream, the direction from which Sammy would have come, pushed along by the river.

They struggled over the rocks, which were slick and wet. Strewn all around were branches and big logs left behind by the water. Morgan couldn't help thinking, Are some of these branches from Sammy's lodge? Did one of these logs crash against the den, breaking it open and sending Sammy down the river?

Morgan and her mother were looking carefully, but could they find another beaver among so much debris?

Rylee and Shire ran around, sniffing and searching. Morgan knew their noses could "see" much better than she could. If there was another baby out here, it would be up to the two dogs to find it.

"You know, we're probably not going to find other animals," Morgan's mother said.

"I know, but I just want to look. It would be scary to be flooded out of your house and left alone."

"Do you ever worry about that? About our house being flooded?"

Morgan nodded slightly. She did, but she didn't want to worry her parents with her fears.

"You know that your father and I would never let anything happen to you, right? We'd leave before the floodwaters reached the house."

"They did reach the porch last year," Morgan said.

"We were safe. We were watching," her mother said.

"But what about when you're sleeping?"

"We listen for reports of the water upstream, and there are police and other people to let us know if we have to evacuate."

"Like they told Emily and her family to leave their house last spring?" Morgan asked.

"Exactly. So you don't have to worry. There are people watching out for all of us."

"I just wish Sammy had some people looking out for him," Morgan said.

"He does...some people plus one very large black dog."

Chapter Six

Morgan let out a big yawn. It had been a long night. She and her parents had taken turns getting up and giving Sammy his bottle, but he'd hardly slept at all. As the night had gone on, Sammy had become more active. Her mother had explained that beavers were nocturnal animals—which meant they liked to sleep during the day and be awake at night. Sammy had cried out for his bottle with humanlike cries, whimpering and chirping. And every time Sammy stirred, both dogs had started up. Shire had whined like he was trying to talk to Sammy, and Rylee had howled to make sure that nobody was going to sleep.

"I had no idea that one little baby could be so much work," Morgan said.

"I'd forgotten myself," her father said. "It's been a long time since *my* baby was a baby." He gave her a big hug.

"Do you think Sammy is going to be all right?" Morgan said.

"He's going to be fine," her mother said.

"The animal-control people will be here soon, and they'll know exactly what to do," her father said. "I'm sure they deal with this sort of thing all the time."

There was a knock on the door. Rylee and Shire started barking and ran for the front door. Morgan's father answered it. Standing there were two men in uniforms.

"Hello. You called for animal control?" one of them asked.

"Yes, we did. Please come in."

The two officers stepped in and then, without being asked, took off their heavy work boots and left them by the door.

"Sorry we couldn't come right away, but things are very busy this time of year," one of the officers said.

"It just gave us more time with Sammy," Morgan's mother said.

"Sammy?" the other officer said.

"That's what we called him. Come and see."

Morgan picked Sammy up out of his box on the floor. He was wrapped in the baby blanket that used to keep her warm when she was little. Morgan had been eager to lend her blanket.

"He certainly is a cutie," the younger of the two officers said.

That made Morgan smile. She offered to let him hold Sammy, and he beamed.

"I've never held a baby beaver before," he said.

"You haven't?" Morgan's father asked.

"Neither have I," said the older officer. "Mostly it's kittens and puppies that we're called for."

"And this time of year we sometimes get raccoon and fox kits, fawns, moose calves and even bear cubs," said the younger officer.

"Bear cubs!" Morgan exclaimed. "You take in bear cubs?"

The older officer shook his head. "We don't have the space or ability to care for the larger animals like bears, deer and moose. We refer those to the Northern Lights Wildlife Society."

"They care for them until they're old enough to be released back into the wild," the younger officer said.

"And that's what you'll do with Sammy?" Morgan asked.

The officers looked uneasy. The older of the two shook his head. "We're not able to do that."

"What do you mean?" Morgan said. "They're easy to care for! You just have to cuddle him and give him a bottle every few hours!"

"We just don't have enough time or people to do that," the older officer explained.

"Then what will happen to Sammy?" Morgan was afraid she already knew the answer.

"I'm sorry, but he'll be put to sleep. I wish there was another way," he said.

"There is!" Morgan took Sammy back from the officer and held him close to protect him. She turned to her parents. "We'll raise him."

Now it was time for her parents to look uneasy. They didn't answer.

"I know it's hard," the officer said. "He's cute right now, but he'll get bigger. It's not like you can raise him in the bathtub or—"

"We can try!" Morgan said. "He can use the bathtub that I use! I don't mind sharing with him!" She burst into tears, and her mother wrapped both arms around her.

"Thanks for coming," Morgan's father said to the officers. "But Sammy will be staying with us."

"We understand," the older officer said. "You can think it over and call us later, and we'll come back."

The two men quietly went to the door, put on their boots and left.

"We're *not* going to call them again...right?" Morgan asked.

"We'll take it one day at a time," her father said. "I'll do the first feeding tonight."

Chapter Seven

When Morgan woke up, her room was bathed in light. She'd slept through the night! What about Sammy? Had her parents called animal control? Had he been taken away? She jumped out of bed and raced down the stairs. Her father was at the stove fixing breakfast and her mother was seated at the table. Sammy was on her lap, holding the bottle with his front legs and using his back legs and tail to hold himself up. Morgan felt a wave of relief. She knew her parents wouldn't have called animal control without telling her, but she had still been afraid.

"I'm so glad to see that he's all right," Morgan said.

"He's fine. I think he's gotten bigger since yesterday," her father said.

"Probably because he's had so many bottles," her mother said.

"But you didn't wake me up to help!"

"We thought you needed your sleep because it was a school night," her father said.

"Not that you're going to school today," her mother added.

"I'm not? Where am I going?"

"We're taking a drive, the three of us...and Sammy."

"Where are we going?" Morgan asked.

"We're going up to the Northern Lights Wildlife Society, the place the officers talked about."

"Would they take Sammy?"

Her father shook his head. "We don't know. We called, but there was no answer. We hope they can at least make a suggestion for what we can do."

Chapter Eight

Morgan had Sammy in a little sling around her shoulder, protected and warm under her jacket. Her parents were in the front seat. Shire had also decided he needed to come along. They'd tried to leave him behind, but he'd barked and chased the car down the road until they finally stopped and let him hop in.

It wasn't that far from their home to the wildlife shelter, but the ride felt long to Morgan. Nobody was talking. The only sounds were Sammy calling out for a bottle and Shire making sure they heard. Sammy snuggled against Morgan. He was warm and dry and fed. She knew he was content now, but he didn't know what was in his future. Nobody knew.

The car slowed down and Morgan looked out the front window. There was a sign—*Northern Lights Wildlife Society*. They had arrived. She suddenly felt even more nervous. They turned up the long driveway. It curved up the hill and through a stand of trees. She could see two buildings, but there weren't any animals in sight. Her mother pulled the car to a stop beside one of the buildings.

A woman came outside. She smiled and waved as they climbed out of the car.

"Hello," the woman called out. "My name is Angelika. My husband and I run the shelter."

"Good morning. I'm sorry for just dropping in," Morgan's mother apologized.

"We tried to call, but we didn't get an answer," Morgan's father added.

"My husband and I just got in. We were on a bear rescue."

They all looked around for a bear—or a husband—but neither appeared.

"My husband is up at the pens, introducing the new cub to the others," she explained.

"How many bear cubs do you have?" Morgan's mother asked.

"With the new cub, we have twelve black bear cubs, along with four moose calves and half a dozen fawns."

"Can we see them?" Morgan asked.

The woman shook her head. "I know it's disappointing, but we only let visitors see the animals twice a year. The rest of the time we try not to allow much contact with humans. It's better for them when we finally release them back into the wild."

"Do you release all the animals you rescue?" Morgan asked.

"That's why we're here," she said.

"And that's what we came to talk to you about," Morgan's father said.

"We brought an animal for you," Morgan said. She opened up her jacket, and Sammy peeked out.

"Is that a little beaver?" the woman gushed.

Morgan nodded her head, and Sammy looked right at Angelika.

"He is so sweet."

"His name is Sammy," Morgan said.

"Hello, Sammy," she said. "You certainly are a handsome little fellow." She stroked Sammy's head, and he let out a tiny chirp.

"How long have you cared for him?"

"Two days," Morgan said.

"And two nights," her father added. "I thought I was done with baby feedings through the night."

"Running the shelter, we'll never be through with those feedings," Angelika said and laughed. "Although we haven't had a beaver here before."

"So you've never rescued a beaver? You've never returned one to the wild?" her father asked.

Angelika shook her head. "Never. I know they need almost constant care, feeding around the clock, and to be held regularly. That would be nearly impossible for us with all the other animals we have to care for."

Morgan felt like her heart was breaking. This was their last hope—*Sammy's* last hope.

"But around here, we often have to do the nearly impossible," she said.

"Do you mean you'll raise him?" Morgan asked.

"We'll try, but we'll need a lot of help," she said. "Do you know of a family, maybe one with a young girl, who would be willing to help us?"

"We could help!" Morgan exclaimed.

Angelika smiled. "I thought you might."

Morgan removed Sammy from the sling. She went to hand him to Angelika and then hesitated, drawing him up to her face. "Don't worry, Sammy, everything is going to be all right. I promise." She passed Sammy over to Angelika.

"Well, Sammy, welcome to your new home. Just don't get too comfortable—you're only here until you're old enough to leave."

Morgan threw her arms around Angelika *and* Sammy. He was home—at least for now.

Afterword

The Northern Lights Wildlife Society is dedicated to giving injured and/or orphaned wildlife a second chance at survival. The society's founders, Angelika and Peter Langen, immigrated to Canada in 1982. Both trained animal keepers, they had previously worked in zoos in Germany. After living in Smithers, British Columbia, for several years, they became aware of the fact that there was no place for injured and/or orphaned wildlife to go to and that such animals ended up being killed.

In 2001 Angelika and Peter formed the NLWS, which became a registered charity the following year. Though all mammals and birds are accepted, the shelter has become a haven for bears, moose and deer. The moose and deer raised at the shelter and released into the nearby park have done extremely well and have proven the success of the program by producing and raising young in the wild year after year.

The NLWS operates solely on the generosity received by its caring donors. Donations are used to cover the cost of rescue missions, veterinary care, feeding and housing during rehabilitation, release expenses and conservation efforts. To find out more about the shelter or learn how you can donate or volunteer, visit www.wildlifeshelter.com.

Author's Note

In the fall of 2012, while on a school tour, my wife and I were hosted by the Monkman family. They told us a story—and showed us pictures—of a little baby beaver that they had found on their property after the river had flooded. They provided for Sammy before turning him over to Angelika and Peter Langen, the founders of the Northern Lights Wildlife Society. Sammy was raised until he was old enough to be released into a wildlife sanctuary. Thanks to the Monkman family for sharing their story with us!

ERIC WALTERS began writing in 1993 as a way to entice his grade-five students into becoming more interested in reading and writing. At the end of the year, one student suggested that he try to have his story published. Since that first creation, Eric has published more than seventy novels. His novels have all become bestsellers and have won over eighty awards. Often his stories incorporate themes that reflect his background in education and social work and his commitment to humanitarian and social-justice issues. He is a tireless presenter, speaking to more than seventy thousand students per year in schools across the country. Eric is a father of three and lives in Mississauga, Ontario, with his wife, Anita, and dogs Lola and Winnie. For more information, visit www.ericwalters.net.